BOSSY FLOSSY

I'm not bossy.

You are bossy.

Paulette Bogan

Henry Holt and Company
NEW YORK

Henry Holt and Company, LLC

Publishers since 1866

175 Fifth Avenue

New York, New York 10010

mackids.com

Library of Congress Cataloging-in-Publication Data

Bogan, Paulette, author, illustrator.

Bossy Flossy / Paulette Bogan. — First edition.

pages   cm

Summary: A bossy girl meets her match.

ISBN 978-1-62779-358-2 (hardback)

[1. Bossiness—Fiction.] I. Title.

PZ7.B6357835Bo 2016   [E]—dc23   2015014261

Our books may be purchased in bulk for promotional, educational, or business use.
Please contact your local bookseller or the Macmillan Corporate and Premium Sales Department
at (800) 221-7945 ext. 5442 or by e-mail at MacmillanSpecialMarkets@macmillan.com.

First Edition—2016 / Designed by April Ward
The artist used watercolors, pens, and colored pencils
in a collage style to make the illustrations for this book.

Printed in China by RR Donnelley Asia Printing Solutions Ltd.,
Dongguan City, Guangdong Province

1 3 5 7 9 10 8 6 4 2

Thank you to my family,
Victoria Wells Arms,
and everyone who helped me—
even when I was being bossy!

She was bossy to her cat.

She was bossy to her little brother.

One time, she was even bossy to her **mother.**

Flossy went to her room.

Flossy was bossy at school.

She was bossy to her classmates.

One time, she was even bossy to her **teacher**.

Flossy went to time-out.

I'm not bossy.

Mrs. Rosado is bossy.

She **always** tells everyone what to do.

They do what she tells them.

Why don't they do what **I** tell them?

Then Flossy met Edward.

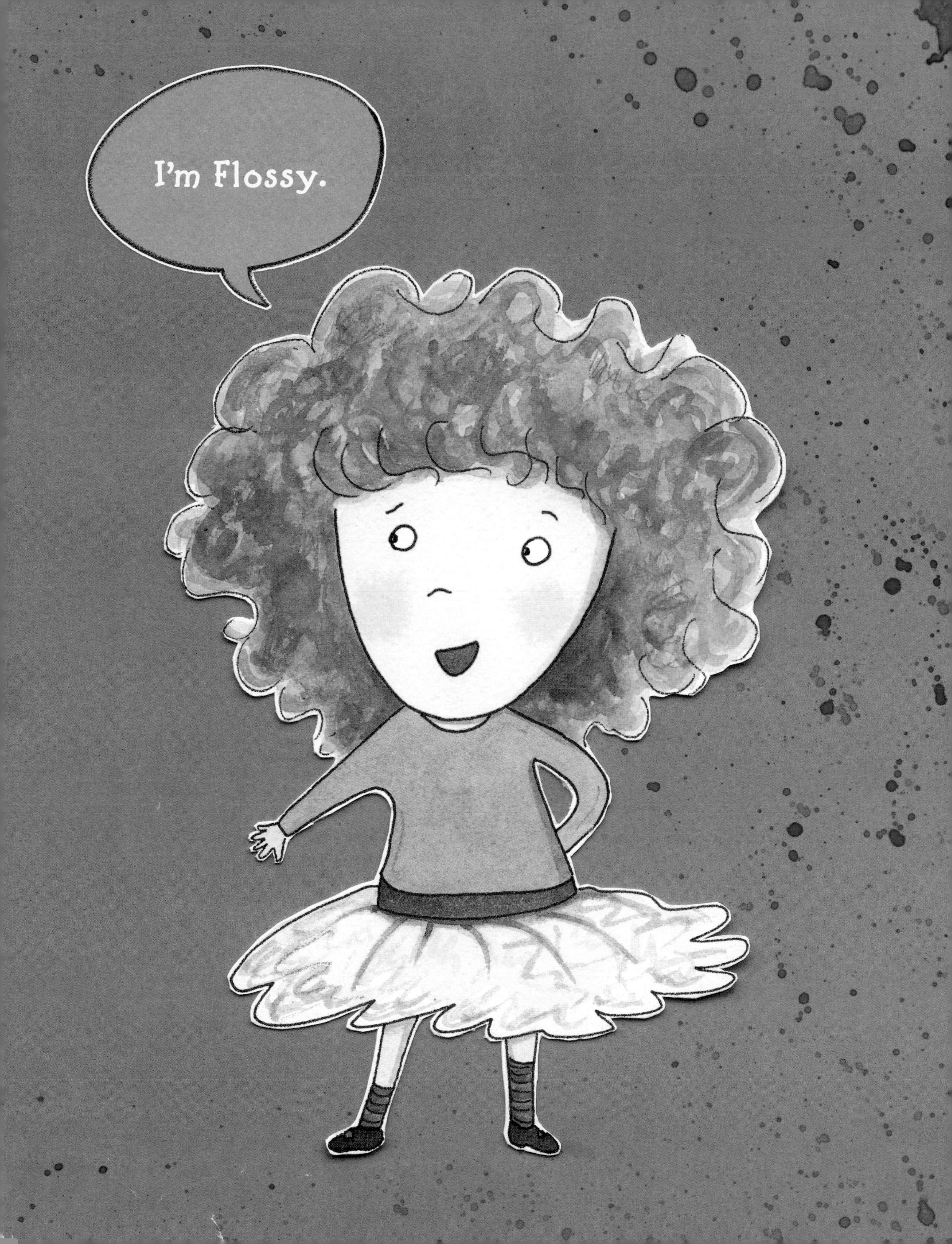
I'm Flossy.

Edward was bossy to everyone.

Edward was even bossy to Flossy.

Flossy got mad.

You are not the boss of me!

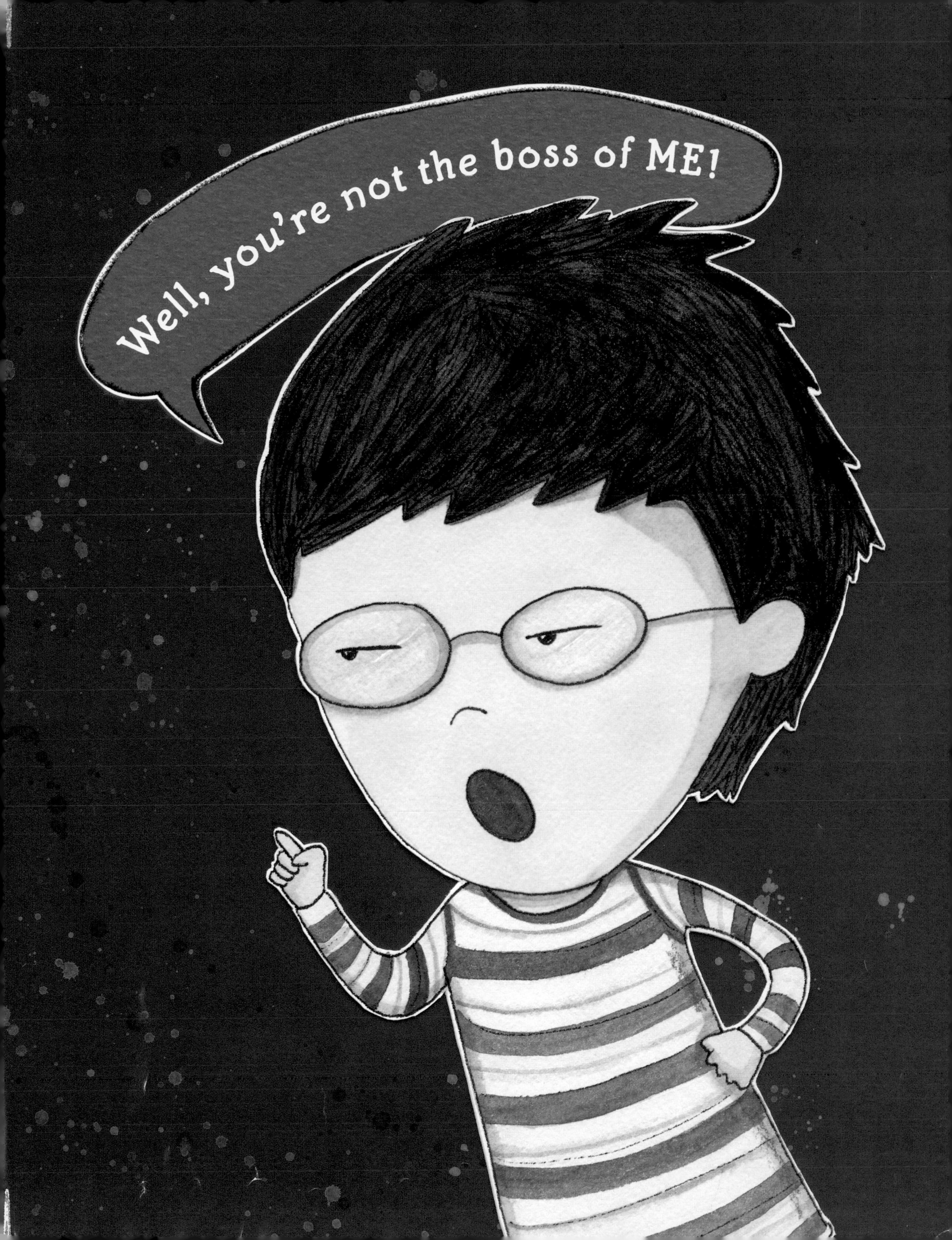
Well, you're not the boss of ME!

Flossy and Edward argued all through art class . . .

and lunch . . .

and nap time.

You **never** listen.
No, **you** never listen!
I'm **trying** to tell you something!

Now Flossy and Edward are not so bossy . . .